The Dolphin
And the
Fisherman

BY LAURIE EMBERSON

Published by Laurie Emberson
9 Harefield Drive, Stoke Fleming, Dartmouth
Devon   TQ6OQG   Tel 01803 771033

This is an account of the adventures of two
creatures of the sea. Both are reaching the end
of their lives and the fears and frustrations
of growing old, in the harsh and demanding
environment of the sea, are common to them both.
They share a fierce pride and stubborn
determination to survive and it is this, which
ultimately brings them together.

This is not an anthropomorphic tale,
only the reader is privy to the thoughts and
emotions of both but the parallels between the
two are clear. We get an insight into both their
worlds and experience the harshness of
nature, where only the young and strong can
survive for long. When they finally meet, a level
of awareness develops between the two in a
struggle to save the life of the old man.

Photograph by Phil Lockley

IN MEMORY OF BOB HOLBORNE, JIM TROUT

AND THE PORTREATH DOLPHIN

For Dianne and all my family

Chapter One

Ola rose to the surface, filling his great lungs with air and spreading his fins wide to hold steady against the roll of the swell. He was exhausted, his body ached with even the slightest movement and the water surface shone like white sand in the sunlight, hurting his eyes. Despite the calm there was little comfort in the rhythm of the waves around him. For the first time in his long life he was alone and suddenly his world seemed a vast and empty place.

The rest of his kind had gone, following the feed shoals south but he was now too old and weak to go with them. In his minds eye the images of his life still shone as bright and sharp as ever but his body was old and tired and he could no longer serve the group.

He floated slowly over the darkness of deep water, suspended in moving columns of dappled sunlight that showed all his grace and form but the scars and damage that marked his age were clearly evident. He turned his hard bottle-nose to the open sea, searching for the sound patterns of his own kind. But only the memory remained and despite his sadness, this last day with the group would be one he would never forget.

That morning, before the sun lit the seabed the dolphins had come for him. With a thrill of excitement, he had felt the smooth shape of young females all around him and the turbulence of their movements across his broad back. One of them had broken from the rest, turning on her side to touch him gently with her fins. Dark questioning eyes filled with compassion, had looked deep into his. It was time.... Resigned, he had turned with her away from the cliffs the others closing in a tight circle around them. As was the custom, the wheel of the group now held him at its centre and would break only when he chose to leave. He had surged forward his tiredness forgotten, almost breaking through the line. They had quickly caught his mood and together, leaping and turning through the waves, they had carried him to the open sea. The group would have run with him as long as he wished, for this was his time. But he was quickly spent and had summoned all his strength for the one last great leap that was expected of him. Up and up he had gone twice his own length clear of the sea, sparkling spray into the sunshine, and end over end with the force of his climb. It had seemed to him that he had reached impossible heights and for a split second his whole life lay before him, far below in the spinning circle of dolphins. Like an arrow through the center of the ring he had dived clean and deep careless of the pain and in the cool dark embrace of mid water, he felt something of the old pride grow within him. Now they would remember him as the dolphin he had always been and forget the feeble creature they must leave behind. For the rest of the day Ola had followed them to the south, running deep below the surface, or riding long ocean swells in the sunlight. Finally, weak with exhaustion, he had stopped tail down in the dim blue light of mid water to send his last contact signal. Slowly the answers had returned, one by one to comfort him. First only faintly then gathering in strength, until familiar overlapping sounds had filled the sea around him and for a moment, for one last moment, he had swum in the heart of the group.

As his breathing slowed and his head began to clear, Ola took stock of his position. He had traveled further than he expected and open water lay on every side. It was only to the north that dark cliffs showed in the distance. Deliberately he quartered the horizon, snapping his jaws together and sending probing signals to scan the distant coast. A hard line of cliffs was quickly revealed to him, broken by small bays and inlets of tumbled rock. Here he might rest and feed in the shallows to recover his strength.

He slipped below the surface and wearily headed for the shore, with slow steady beats of his muscular tail. Dark cliffs against the evening sky stretched long shadows towards him as he approached, running low over the seabed a shadow among shadows. Fine clouds of debris lifted from the tide ridged white sand as he passed. Cautiously he scanned ahead as the water shallowed, every detail of the rocky coast etched in his minds eye. Two great rocks loomed before him, towering to the surface and a canopy of swirling kelp fronds filled the narrow space between. Knuckles of armoured barnacles sharp enough to cut his tough hide, showed through the soft weed but at the seabed the rock was bare, worn smooth by tide and shifting sand.

Ola rolled his great bulk and slipped between the rocks, surfacing in a small sheltered bay beneath towering cliffs. He breathed thankfully, clearing his lungs with an echoing cry. Startled seabirds tumbled into flight from the ledges above shrieking with alarm as they vanished into the sky. The dolphin ignored them filling his great lungs with sweet fresh air. He was exhausted, tired beyond hunger, wanting only to rest and recover his strength. When the sun rose again, there would be time enough to think of food. The last of the tide spilled through the narrow entrance of the bay and turned him gently into the quiet water at its center, surrounding him with a thousand familiar sounds to comfort and reassure. Above him, the ledges filled again with roosting birds.

Beyond Ola's hidden cove the cliffs curved to the west giving way to a long sweeping bay. The warm rain of early summer had washed the headland clean and yellow celandines and blackthorn blossom covered the scars of winter.

Within the bay the broken walls of an old fishing village stood among the rocks. It backed a narrow shingle beach and a small cottage nestled above it over the ruins, Its clay tiled roof bright in the setting sun. A tiny flower garden spread like an apron before it and a single column of white smoke rose from the chimney into the clear blue sky.

On the beach close to the water, the dark clad figure of an old man stood beside a small fishing boat. He lived alone in the cottage above the sea and he was the last in a long line of fisher folk who had lived in the village for generations. When he was a boy, dredging ships had come to the bay and taken the shingle banks of the seabed and with them had gone the village defenses against the sea. One by one the houses had fallen to winter storms until the people had lost heart and moved away and the village and community and the way things had been was forgotten, except in the heart of the old man.

Malcolm Luscombe leant heavily on the side of his boat and pushed himself upright, turning towards the sea. He lifted his cap letting the breeze cool the sweatband and dry his thinning white hair. His hands were large and strong and he held his head high like a man who knew his mind and his pale green eyes sunk deep in a gaunt weathered face, were unblinking in the bright sunlight. He scanned the bay with professional interest. High cirrus cloud promised another day of good weather and the quiet water it would bring, meant he could haul the last of his pots the following day.

His pots had been on the seabed for a week and the bait inside them would be gone by now. If he did not look lively any lobsters he may have caught would abandon them. He pursed his lips and frowned picturing the creatures climbing out of his funnel traps to freedom then shrugged and grinned. There was no sense in thinking like that. There would be something there or not, when the time came and he could have got to sea no sooner. Bad weather earlier in the week had seen to that plus the two days lost nursing that damned engine back to life. He scowled at the thought of his work on the engine. He mistrusted anything mechanical and still missed the old Lug-sail rig under which he and his brother used to sail. But that was all in the past, when they were young men and the ways of the modern world had not yet reached them. John had been right to abandon sail when he did and they had prospered with the change. But, the old man thought wistfully, if only his brother were still here to look after that engine.

The old man looked up quickly as colour flashed in the sunlight. Petals of blue and white and red, rode the gentle breeze from the ocean and brought a smile again to the old man's face. They were butterflies, carried from the continent, making their summer landfall on the Devon coast.

"Them's early this year" The old man said.

He spoke aloud, as a man alone often did, in the soft dialect of his kind.   "Tis a good sign"

He replaced his cap and pulled it down square over his eyes as he watched the bright gossamer wings spin and dip towards him across the bay. At the surf line they lifted and scattering like broken flower heads in the up draught of the land and in a moment they were gone, lost in a tangle of blackthorne and gorse. At his feet the sea lay quiet in the low sunlight with only a hiss and rattle of pebbles...The old man grunted his approval. The beauty of the bay was never lost on him but he was no casual observer. He was part of the fabric of this landscape. Living and working on the very edge of man's world. Nature was a hard mistress and like the birds of the cliffs and the creatures of the sea, he must understand her moods and read them well to survive. It was not that he thought of nature as merciless or cruel but experience had taught him any carelessness was not easily forgiven. He turned back to his labours.

Willow pots glistening, still wet from the sea, lay tumbled in the open boat. Barnacles covered their battered wooden frames and weeded rope twisted around them into unnatural coils. He reached down and crooked fingers into a sodden frame, his hard angular body taking the strain with practiced ease. He swung the pot clear of the gunwale and carried it over the soft shingle beach to firmer ground. He had found the string only that morning. Spotting the top marker a foot below the surface with red weed flowing like a girl's hair in the tide. It had been lost for some time and he counted himself lucky to get it back. The pots would need repair for sure, but there would be time enough for that when the easterly wind blew and there was no fishing. The old man had worked the bay all his life with his brother John. Potting for crab and lobster off the point and netting salmon and mullet through long summer evenings. It had been a hard life but he had known no other and had few regrets. He dropped the last pot onto the shingle, carefully coiling the top rope around it. As it ran between his hands, he rubbed it against a palm, hard as leather. Beneath the encrusted shell and weed, the turns shone white and clean in the soft light. He thought. It was good for more seasons than he was, but he quickly brushed the thought aside and straightened his back, easing his stiffness.

"Enough of that". He growled.

Tired muscles and aching joints were the price to pay for still being here and it was nothing he couldn't handle. But the recent loss of his brother had weakened him and it was a harsh reminder of his own mortality.

"Anyhow, us did well enough today." He said defensively.

He nodded his head with conviction. There is many a youngster wouldn't have hauled that extra string after a full days work, he thought. Not the way youngsters are today, that's for sure. He shook his head emphatically and bent to pick up a rusting winch wire, clipping it onto the bow. The tide was falling and as the water left his boat, the 'Mary Jane' settled her worn underbelly onto the soft weed of the tide line. He gathered up rope ends tied to greased planks from the top of the beach and dragged them down to the boat, pushing one beneath the bow and spacing the others up the beach under the line of the winch wire. Hauling the boat over the planks was kind to the hull and made it easier for him to haul her up. But it was all becoming increasingly hard. He spat into his hands and rubbed them together, moving slowly up the beach. The wire from the boat ran to a snatch block in the cliff and then followed the path at right angles to the winch high above the shoreline. The winch had been in use for as long as the old man could remember. In the early days, it was mounted at the foot of the cliff, where grass and bracken bound the shingle firm. It had been safe and dry there through the worst of winter storms but after the dredging nature had exacted a terrible revenge. Within twenty years the beach was gone and most of the village and the winch lay buried under rotting weed. Only the old man and his brother remained to pull it out of the shingle and drag it to safety. He had not wanted to bother. It was bigger than the two of them would ever need. But John had laughed grimly and said they should and that he must remember that the winch and the two of them was all that was left.

The old man slowly climbed the cliff path thankfully pausing for breath at the winch. He rested his shoulder for a moment against the rusting iron wheel. Below him thin grass and bramble gave way to the rocks of the foreshore and the broken walls of the old village framed his boat on the narrow beach.

He lent forward, clutching the wheel looking down beyond the cliff edge to the high water mark. There was no more than twenty feet of beach left at the foot of the cliff and he knew that one big blow next winter could scour the shingle from between the rocks and his beach and his livelihood would be gone forever.

"Oh well"

The old man shrugged and lowered himself stiffly down beside the winch. Pushing his cap over his eyes and scratching his head.

"I recon I am about ready to pack in; come the end of the season I will have had enough, whether the sea comes up or not."

Malcolm smiled, thinking himself an old fool to dwell on such things, on a beautiful summer day. But somehow it was days like this when the weather was fair and the fishing good that the memories of the old times came flooding back. The broken path and the tumbled ruins told precious little of what had been here when the beach was strong. In those days, forty fishermen had worked their boats from a great beach that stretched way out beyond Wilson's rock. Malcolm closed his eyes and let familiar sounds and smells invade his senses. On such an evening as this the beach would be alive with the sounds of the village. The old ford engine on the winch would be heard, clearing its throat for the haul and the voices of the women folk calling to their men at the waters edge. Smoke from the chimneys below would bring the smell of coal fire and cooking, all the way up to the cottage.

The old man sighed and turned to the job in hand. It did not do to dwell too much in the past. There was little comfort in it, he thought. Not now, with John gone. Not like it was when the two of them would sit before a fire on long winter evenings. Now that was a rare time for bringing the old days to life!

Grasping the wooden sleeve of the winch handle he turned it slowly to take up the slack on the wire. The cogs grated and squealed, as his muscles took the strain of the boat. Below the "Mary Jane" stirred and lifted her bow. The old man spread his feet and threw his weight against the wheel. With relief, he felt the pressure ease as the boat slid onto the greased timbers. And he began to count the turns of the wheel, as he always did.

"One…two…Three…Four…Five."

One hundred turns would bring her to the winch block and safely above high water. He thought. I will do fifty and then rest. There is no point in doing it in one, if I don't have to.

"Not that I couldn't mind." The old man said, and grinned to himself. But he was alone now. What did he have to prove.? By the time the 'Mary Jane' was safely tucked beneath the cliff, the sun was gone from the beach and the path to his cottage lay in soft shadow. It was only a short distance but the old man waited until his heart was quiet and his breathing sound before attempting the climb.

The path was steep and overgrown and roots worn and polished by hiker's boots formed natural steps to ease his climb towards the sunlight. He always enjoyed this, when the beach was cool and the sea had lost its sparkle and he could climb up into the warmth and light of the cliff top. It was a good feeling. The old man felt the strain on his heart and breathed harshly through clenched teeth but he did not stop to rest until he reached the footpath below the wall of his cottage.

His home was a simple affair its rough walls built of local stone and shingle from the beach and high enough above the salt line for the small garden to provide the vegetables he needed. It had caused some amusement among the fishermen when his grandfather had chosen a site so far from the beach but events had proved it to be a wise decision.

The cottage was set into the hillside in a cushion of elder bushes and blackthorn, with a small slate porch at the side to keep the southeast winds from the house. There had been a low wooden fence marking the area of the land but in latter years the brothers had wearied of repair and abandoned it and allowed the brier and blackthorn into the garden. There were few visitors these days, welcome or unwelcome. But cliff walkers sometimes passed by and if they found John in his garden they would stop, with their map boards and books of local information and engage him in conversation; if they could. The questions were always the same. Was he here during the troubles and what was it like.... and how did he manage in the winter? For the most part John would turn his back and pretend not to hear but if the mood took him he would walk a little way along the path with them, his cap pushed back and his great arms folded across his chest and talk to them and tell them about the village and how it was to be a young man among fishermen, in the old days.

With a grunt of relief the old man sat down on the narrow bench within the porch, to recover his breath. He dropped his cap beside him and kicked off his clumsy thigh boots, stretching his legs and leaning back against the cool slate. He closed his eyes and listened to his heart as it laboured from the climb and felt the dull ache of its strain slowly pass. He could smell the honeysuckle that clung to the porch frame and feel the gentle breeze from the sea, cooling his brow. He would sit here for a few minutes, he thought, as he always did. Until he felt better, or the need for a cup of tea became too strong. Then he would go in.   It was quiet inside the cottage. Even with the open door he could scarcely hear the gulls, or the sea on the rocks below. It had been just such a day when his brother had died. The old man shook his head and tried to push the thought from his mind but there was much to remind him. His brother's boots still stood in the porch. His coat and cap hung beside them and through the open kitchen door he could see the bare pine table and the edge of the chair, where John always sat. The mantle clock beat like a heart in the stillness. It was as if life was still here and nothing had changed and through the window above the table, the view of the lighthouse hung like a painting, impossibly white against the blue evening sky. He moved into the kitchen and took a box of matches from the wooden shelf and lit the small stove. Dropping the lighted match onto the stone floor he gazed thoughtfully into the gas flame, remembering that last day and once more feeling a sense of guilt with his loss.

If only he could have known it was to be his brothers last, he would have stayed home and done the best he could to look after him and perhaps made a difference. A man's last day ought to mean something. He thought of the things he might have said to comfort John, things his brother might have wanted to hear. But there had been nothing to tell the

18

old man there was anything amiss that morning. They had shared breakfast as they always did with little passing between them. Neither of them ever had much to say in the early mornings. His brother had not even answered when he said goodbye. He was sitting at the table and just raised a hand without looking round, as he left.

The old man shook his head. It was as if in the scheme of things, a man's life was of no importance at all and it did not matter whether there was anyone with him to comfort him at the end. He could just slip away unnoticed.

Perhaps his brother had been right all along. John always said that people made too much of themselves. Why should a human life be any more important, than a fish caught from the sea or a bird that died on the cliff top? But John was like that. He would say things with a smile and you were never sure whether he meant it, or what he was really thinking. But if he did mean it and he was right, the old man reasoned then it didn't matter leaving things unsaid, or trying to find some meaning to it all. On his return to the cottage that day, everything had seemed normal enough. He had found his brother sleeping peacefully in his chair. One arm across the table fingers spread, the other wrapped around his ample stomach.

He was a large and powerful man and even in old age the aura of strength was still with him. He slept head forward on his barrel chest snoring softly into his sweater. It was stained and patched from years at sea and the sleeves were pushed back to the elbows in the manner of a working fisherman. But it had been six months since he had been to sea and wrist ulcers and rope burns, had faded and healed and the skin of his arms had paled. It was as if the sea knew he would never return and had already given him up. As the old man watched his brother sleeping, undecided whether to wake him or not, he had heard a flutter of sound and turned to find a herring gull on the step of the open door behind him. It had stood, quite still, head on one side as if deciding whether or not to enter and had ignored him completely. The old man's surprise had turned to unease, as its yellow ringed eye fixed on his brothers still form. As it watched John's breathing became weak and shallow, with a bubbling sound like that of a child. And the last breath when it came was a low sigh impossibly long, from the depth of his body. He had moved quickly to his brother's side but as he reached out to touch him, there was a barely susceptible movement. A crumbling of the body into itself and the hand in his lap had opened slowly, palm upwards, as if to free the soul. In the silence that followed the old man heard the bird again. He looked up to see its shadow in the room as it spread its wings and lifted from the step. It hung for a moment floating silently on the up-draught from the cliff and rose slowly until it was lost from view. He had followed its path with his eyes across the low stained ceiling, until he saw it again at the window, soaring high above the ridge to the headland and the sea.

The old man moved the kettle quietly over the flame. The presence of the bird at his brother's death had affected him profoundly and he would never forget it and he felt in his heart, despite his doubts that his brother's spirit had gone with the gull that day and that John had been wrong and a life, any life was important and no one should ever die alone.

Chapter Two

Ola slept soundly and woke at low tide, his pool now only a shallow basin of swirling water and weed. The birds had left the ledges and above the cliffs, gulls wheeled and called hungry voices in the bright morning sunshine. In the distance he heard the cry of a seal.

The sea sucked and gurgled restlessly around him. Weed stems over sharp rocks brushed his soft stomach urging him to leave. Ola shook his bulk from the clinging kelp and slipped out of the bay into deeper water.

He was hungry. A school of bass running with the tide, swept over him, vanishing into the gloom. His fins twitched in response, his pulse quickening with the though of a chase but he made no move to follow. They were too fast for him to catch.

Ola glided watchfully across a reef, his bulk all but invisible against the dark rocks. He knew he would need all his cunning to catch even the slowest prey.

Turning his head from side to side, he sifted familiar sounds and tastes beyond his vision. Hard mouthed reef fish scrapped at shell covered rocks. Crabs and shrimps and a hundred tiny creatures clicked and whispered in kelp forest shadows. Above him, diving birds drummed their hunting song on fin-like wings through the surface water. Ola vented a stream of bubbles and sank into the kelp sending a cautious signal ahead. He quickly discovered what was attracting the diving birds. A pattern of sound reflected back from a shoal of sand eels slowly moving towards him with the tide. The eels were a small meal for him but larger prey might well be circling under the shoal.

Concealed in the weed, Ola steadied his body against the roll of the tide, twitching his great tail with anticipation. The water above the forest was clear and bright emerald green in the morning sunshine. The eels approached him, a shifting column of tiny creatures, suspended above the reef.

The dolphin sensed the movement of larger fish in the weed below the shoal, his heart jumped with excitement but the kelp that concealed him so well made a quick strike all the more difficult. A bold approach would give him his best chance.

Driving for the surface with all his strength, Ola burst into the sunlight and the path of the startled birds. Eels broke in confusion as he crashed back into the sea, arrowing through the shoal to his prey below. In an instant he was among them snapping to right and left, his hard nose brushing the tails of fleeing fish as he spun out of his dive. But for all his efforts he was too slow and in a moment his prey was gone.

Weak and shaken with the effort, Ola sank tail first to the edge of the reef onto soft white sand. Above him in the debris of his trail the fish shoals quickly reformed, teasing him with their indifference and dark shadows dipped and flickered around him as the diving birds returned.

It was some time before Ola felt well enough to move. He pushed himself from the seabed and rose slowly to the surface, trying to clear his dulled senses in the fresh air. With dismay, he realised his strength was returning more slowly than he could ever remember. He rolled in a gentle swell, his eyes closed against the bright sun. He felt suddenly very old and tired. Emptying his lungs, Ola sank slowly back to the seabed his heavy bulk settling into comforting soft sand. A silver cloud of tiny bubbles reached to the surface above. A shimmering screen between him and the next breath...If he chose to take it!

Ola considered, as if he was no longer part of the tired old body that lay there. It was as if death was close by; he could feel it, but there seemed little to fear. Perhaps fear was only for the young and strong with so much to lose? Suddenly Ola saw what he had become. He was an exhausted old creature with only his pride for companion, trying to prove that nothing had changed and he could still do what he had always been able to. Weakly he shook his head burying his bulk into the soft sand. A white curtain of suspended crystals lifted and slowly settled over his still form.

The turn of the tide lifted Ola, moving him on his bed of sand and he became aware of form taking shape among the dark rocks before him. He looked up as the water began to clear, sensing movement in soft colours above waving kelp. He tensed, lifting painfully onto his pectoral fins. A large sand ray dropped toward him carried on the tide. Ola lay motionless as the creature glided towards him but he moved not a muscle. With a flurry of wing tips the ray buried into the seabed.

Hunger overcame all caution and Ola threw his great body forward with all the strength he could muster, trapping the fish under his hard nose. In a moment it was gripped fast in his strong jaws.

He would eat at last! All thoughts of giving up were now forgotten in his moment of triumph. His doubts seem to vanish with the meal and his heart beat more strongly. Life was still sweet, he thought. It was still precious. All he had needed was a full stomach to give him the will to fight and the strength to go on. He shook himself free of the sand in a stream of bubbles, following them slowly to the surface to breathe. He had learnt a good lesson. He would hunt the prey that hid not the fish that ran!

In the days that followed Ola worked hard to develop new hunting skills in a world where creatures relied on camouflage and stealth not speed to survive. It was nothing new for him to hunt fish that lived in the sand. He and the other dolphins would furrow the soft seabed with their heavy noses driving eels and small flat fish before them into a circle, where confused and helpless, few would escape. But, for an old dolphin working alone, it was different. Somehow he must avoid the chase and in so doing save his strength. Quickly he began to recognize the feeding grounds and food of his likely prey, shrimps and small shellfish in the debris between rocky groins. Worm cast piles, pushed up on the sand, attracting hungry flat fish and the soft sand at the edge of the reefs where ray and plaice would bury and rest after a meal. At night, when the shallows were lit only by the moonlight, Ola would hide up and wait for the rays to swim in from deep water. Grey ghosts on silent wings, climbing the coastal shelves to their feeding grounds; here the rays would hunt until dawn. Their sharp noses digging out worms and shellfish from the soft sand...

Here too the hunters became the hunted.

As Ola's confidence grew so he moved further afield in his search for food and to his delight he found he could still surprise wrasse and mullet among the rocks and gulleys in shallow water. Life was good again and gave Ola a renewed sense of strength and purpose. All he wished for now was companionship and even this was to be granted to him but from a most unlikely quarter.

He was hunting in the shallows at high tide on the edge of the kelp forest, when suddenly a large plaice lifted from between the rocks into open water. It escaped his jaws in a flurry of sand, disappearing into the kelp. Undecided, Ola circled for a moment watching the sand plume that marked its trail. Finally curiosity got the better of him and he nosed cautiously into the thick brown fronds of the upper forest. Kelp clung to his fins and tail as he pushed through into a narrow gulley below. Sunlight filtered the canopy dappling the rocks and sand with a flickering golden hue; quite unlike anything Ola had seen before. He vented air to increase his weight and settled into a sand corridor; it was a narrow path between rocks that stretched ahead of him into the forest. Weed stalks on knobbed feet grew from the high rocks on either side forming a canopy above. Their fronds swept back and forth with the restless movement of the sea.

Protected from the scouring of tides and currents the rock walls around him shone with tiny flowering life forms. Fish shoals crowded the weed stems and bright coloured wrasse swayed with the tide secure in the canopy above.

The dolphin was intrigued but cautious at being so confined. He moved slowly forward over the white sand, careful of the kelp stalks on either side. All around him was the secret life of the forest. Pale flat fish, some he had never seen before, hid in the sand among the reed stems. Spotted plaice, camouflaged among sponge-covered rocks, darted into the kelp at his approach and bright-eyed dogfish lay still and watchful as he passed. As he moved further into the forest the rock faces increased in height on either side, the canopy rising above him. No longer confined he could now swim again and rolling onto his side he glided over the rock face. Jewel anemones sparkled in the filtered sunlight among fronds of brightly coloured weed and a silver path of tiny fish emerged to follow him.

Suddenly, Ola sensed another presence, a heavy body in the canopy above. He stopped tail down, lifting his head defensively his hard nose penetrating the kelp, ready to break from the confines of the gulley if need be. He felt the surge of the tide against his pectoral fins as he lifted slowly into the kelp line. All at once the fronds were thrust aside and two large brown eyes framed in a dark whiskered face peered down at him. A moment later the round speckled body of a young seal tumbled past him through the canopy into the gulley below. It hung for a moment before him, then doubled over onto its back and dived into the weed stems. Its sinewy body twisted and turned through the kelp in its effort to escape.

Ola's curiosity got the better of him and he decided to follow. Pushing up through the canopy into open water, he swam slowly over the tell tale line of bubbles left by the baby seal. He had no wish to frighten the little creature further so he kept his distance but it was clearly distressed and he was surprised to find one so young, apparently alone. There had been no storms or violent seas recently that might have separated a group. Ola waited, his dark shadow floating above the weed. The bubbles had stopped but he knew exactly where the creature was. A pattern of sound signals clearly outlined the tiny form in the forest below. Suddenly the young seal burst into view mouth agape, driving hard for the surface, thrusting into the air like a newborn dolphin struggling for its first breath. Ola was anxious not to frighten the creature further and surfaced a little distance away. The seal hung upright, working hard to keep its small head clear of the water. It sucked noisily through its mouth and nose and rolled terrified eyes in his direction.

Scanning the small wasted form, Ola felt the beating of a heart, so like a dolphin's, it re-awakened painful memories of his own kind. He moved closer. The seal lifted itself high out of the water and cried out. A shrill plaintive sound, cut short as the creature sank below the surface. A thin stream of bubbles marked its trail in the clear water. Ola dived quickly, driving hard with tail and pectoral fins, to catch the seal before it reached the kelp. Gently he slipped his bottlenose under the soft belly, grasping one of its clawed flippers in his mouth. Slowly he carried the seal back to the surface.

A sea breeze was blowing fresh from the land, breaking white-topped waves across Ola's broad back. He turned away, shielding the baby seal, supporting it on his pectoral fin. It struggled and broke free, slipping back into the water. To Ola's surprise it now made no attempt to swim away but clung to him with its sharp claws. He did his best to support it and lay still as it scrambled onto his broad head. He turned carefully into the wind and fine spray broke over them both, as he headed slowly for the shore.

It was the dolphin's intention to leave the seal in the rocky shallows where it would be safe. Other seals must be in the area and its cries for help would soon be answered. Gulls circled above them as they approached the cliffs spiralling down to drop lightly on either side with shrill warning cries. The young seal lifted its head, adding its own anguished cries to that of the birds but clinging tightly to the dolphin. Sheltered from the wind Ola turned in the shadow of the cliffs, searching for a place for the seal to land. Flat-weeded ledges at the waterline glistened under a breaking swell. Below water, the reef rose as sheer as the cliffs above, from a forest of kelp. It was no place to leave the seal. Ola turned and followed the cliff line until he came upon a small headland and more sheltered water. Here the weeded heads of great rocks touched the surface with swirling fingers and the dark mouth of a cave rose before them. The water at its mouth was smooth and quiet. Cautiously Ola approached and slipped inside. The cave was deep and Ola's probing signal into the darkness showed a high vaulted roof and a tumble of rocks at its centre. It would do well enough. Ola's fin cut a white swirl on the black surface as he pushed the seal towards the rocks. Inside the cliff the familiar sounds of surf and gulls were lost. Only the shallow breath of the sea as it surged through the cave mouth echoed from the walls around them. The seal dragged itself panting from the water bright eyes shining in the dim light. Ola moved clear floating in the deeper water of the cave. He should leave but he hesitated. Perhaps drawn to the young creatures needs by his loneliness. Those limpid eyes had re-awakened old memories of life with his group. He remembered once again the warm sun of past years upon his back and the power of the group around him. In the deep water below he saw the dark shapes of pregnant females moving with attendant dolphins. All around the call of the birth song, gathering in strength as the time came... A tiny form flashing in the aqua marine, would race for the surface, to gasp its first breath in the water beside him. Then it would be gone, spinning in a cloud of spray to a waiting mother below.

In the cave, Ola was suddenly aware the seal had slipped back into the water and swum to his side. He felt its noisy breathing, warm against him. It cried, with a soft mewing sound, reaching up to gently explore his smooth skin with its soft whiskered nose. It was close enough to weaning to remember its mother's milk. Ola spread a pectoral fin and gently pushed the creature away, back towards the rocks. It twisted round clawing at him, eyes big and reproachful. But it was time for him to leave.

Breaking away from the seal he moved out of the dark cave mouth and dived into the kelp forest. White sand lifting in fine clouds through the canopy was all that marked his path. He surfaced clear of the forest in open water, where a gentle wind from the land petalled the surface, white against the setting sun. The cave mouth had vanished in the shadow of the rocks but as Ola lifted his head, he glimpsed a small dark shape on the smooth water; the baby seal was following. He watched as cliff shadows lengthened over the sea, the sun now almost gone. The seal faltered and began to circle. It had clearly lost his trail and there was little chance of it finding him in the failing light... A thin anguished cry carried across the water. Ola slipped below the surface and dived into the gloom of mid water. He turned at the seabed and sent a signal towards the surface and the cliffs, hoping the seal had turned back to the cave. A picture of sound showed a small round shape against the sky and a softly beating heart. All thoughts of leaving the seal vanished with the contact and Ola surfaced beside it to the obvious delight of the little creature.

With his young charge in tow, Ola's passage was a slow and gentle swim on the surface. He was glad of the rest, tired from his exertions and resolved to return to the security of his cove. Shielded from the breaking seas, the seal swam close beside him as naturally as if the dolphin had been one of its own. It seemed content to put its trust in him.

It was high tide when they slipped into the cove and the water was silver under a full moon. Ola spread his fins and dropped his tail in rest. His companion moved close and was quickly asleep beside him. It was good to be back, and not alone, he thought. He listened to the others gentle breathing and drifted into a sleep of memories, to the comforting feel of another heartbeat.

Ola woke as first light touched the dark cliffs above them and gulls began to stretch their wings in early flight. The pool was shallow again and stirring restlessly with weed fronds touching the surface. The seal lay close to him supported by the dolphin's broad fin. It lay with its head above the surface mouth wide, snoring noisily in complete abandon. Ola pulled his fin sharply away tumbling the animal into the water. The little creature sank beneath him but quickly re-appeared wide-eyed and choking, only to be pushed up onto the rocks by the dolphin. Ola slapped his tail hard on the water to prevent the seal rejoining him and the sound lifting every bird from the ledges, wheeling into the air in protest. His meaning was clear and the young seal stayed where it was. Ola was hungry and it was best he hunted alone. There were two mouths to feed now and without the seal, more chance of a catch. There would be time enough for the pup to join him in the hunting when its strength returned.

The sky was grey and heavy with cloud as the dolphin left the pool and the sea had a different rhythm. There was a change coming, Ola could feel it. He lifted his head clear of the surface, his thoughts with the young seal. If a storm came from the sea there would be little protection for them here. Ola dived to the edge of the forest, turning into the tide. His fins brushed the sand, his hard nose cutting a narrow trench across the seabed. A large plaice, disturbed by his burrowing, shook of its sand camouflage and prepared for flight. Ola caught it quickly carrying it to mid water before satisfying his hunger. The meal refreshed him and he returned at once to the sand to catch a small dab for his companion.

On his return to the cove Ola found the seal on the weed strewn rocks where he had left it. He called it into the water, imitating the pup's high-pitched cry. The tide was beginning to rise again but the pool was still little more than a bed of kelp. Uncomfortably shallow for a creature of Ola's size. The seal seemed confused by the small fish in Ola's mouth. Unsure what was expected of him; Ola bit it in two and shook his head scattering the pieces into the water. Still the creature did nothing but snuffle at them with his delicate nose. In desperation Ola began chewing on one of the larger pieces and all at once the seal understood. Grasping the food on the claw of one flipper it tore at the fish, throwing its head back and gulping it down. In a moment the fish was gone and mewing with delight, the little creature began tugging at the dolphin's jaw. Ola opened his cavernous mouth wide and the seal peered inside, seemingly unabashed by the rows of shining teeth. Finding there was nothing more to be had, it pushed away from him and disappeared into the weed bed. The path of the baby seal was plain to see in the carpet of weed and Ola marvelled at the antics of its muscular little body. It twisted and flowed as supple as the weed stems surfacing before him with a crown of fronds, to shake free and sink again without a ripple. Clearly it had recovered its strength and confidence. It was time to teach it to hunt. Slipping through the tunnel of weed to the white sand, he waited for the seal to join him and swam slowly into the sunlight of mid water. The young seal held station above Ola's head constantly swimming to the surface to breath but returning swiftly as if fearful of loosing its new companion. Intent on showing the seal how to catch its own food, Ola was reluctant to feed it again himself. He dived to the seabed and sped across the white sand his hard nose lifting a cloud of sediment for the seal to follow. His probing signals searched ahead for the hard outline of his prey. A small buried plaice sleeping in the sand, gave him the opportunity he needed. Only its eyes and pectoral fin was visible above the seabed. Balanced on tail and fins, Ola waited motionless for the seal to join him. Only when he was aware of his companion close beside him in the gloom, did the dolphin move. Gently Ola lifted his great bulk over his prey, dropping his jaw to trap the fish on the seabed. A cloud of sand trailing back from his head with the tide, obscured the water but as it cleared the seal became aware of the struggling fish beneath Ola's jaw. Slipping under his fins, perilously close to being crushed by the dolphin's bulk, he grasped the plaice by the tail, shaking it from side to side. Obligingly Ola released his captive, which at once tore itself free from the clutches of the seal and fled. In close pursuit the seal followed its every twist and turn, over the kelp forest high into the blue mid water above Ola's head and low onto the rolling sand of open ground. Finally in a desperate attempt to escape, the exhausted fish doubled back into its own sand trail and was caught fast in the seal's sharp claws.

Ola rejoined the seal on the surface among rolling wave tops. It was already intent on eating its catch and was tearing the fish apart and gulping it down, with great speed. It barked a cry of welcome as the dolphin appeared, clutching the remains of the fish to its chest and racing through the waves to meet him. Ola was well pleased. Clearly he need have few worries now, on the seal's behalf. It would soon be able to fend for its self. However other thoughts were beginning to occupy his mind. The change he had sensed in the weather was almost upon them.

Seaward of the dolphin's cove, beyond Cherrick rocks, the underwater scene was as harsh and exposed as the headland above. Where wind torn stunted oak and gorse gave way to the sea, a canopy of kelp weed, covered the rocks and thrust eastwards into Ola's world. This shallow reef was a haven for sea creatures when the wind was light, or blowing from the west. But the wind that was coming was from the open ocean to the south and the seas it would bring, would penetrate deep into the kelp forest and scour the gulleys to the sandy floor. This would be a time when the sea would threaten every living creature. When rock-fish, crab and lobster must hold fast, deep within caves and crevasses and shoal fish and dolphin alike must leave for calmer waters.

Chapter Three

First came the swell, lifting from the south, with just a draught of wind. It broke on the low rocks of the headland, reforming and lifting at the foot of the cliffs. It washed gull-soiled rocks and freshened stagnant pools softening high water weed, drying in the wind. It told the birds that thronged the cliffs of the change that was coming and it ran a warning finger along the hard edge of the bay.

The old fisherman turned his boat up into the wind, moving his weathered face from side to side to pin point its direction. With one hand resting lightly on the tiller, he pushed back his cap to scratch at his brow and frowned, pale eyes narrowing as he gazed thoughtfully ahead. On the horizon the sea and sky had become one, dark and menacing. The wind was light enough but the swell from the open sea brought its own message. There was bad weather out in the ocean and the old man knew that it would soon be with him. He had tried to raise all his gear the day before. He had read the signs and had known what was coming. But trying to haul all his pots and get them safely ashore, had tired him beyond the point of safety and like it or not, he had been forced to leave work for the following day. He opened the throttle and steered the 'Mary Jane's broad bow seaward, over the heavy swell. She pitched and rolled and a wave broke over her, as he turned into the wind. Salt water stung his eyes and wetted his faded smock and washed his boots but he paid no heed. There was no way a fisherman ever kept dry at sea. He grinned wryly to himself and tucked the discomfort away in his mind as he always did.

The old man glanced over his shoulder to his landmarks on the ridge. The cottage on the headland was in line with the south end of the village, as it should be. In just a few minutes on this course, the Blackstone rock would cover Peartree point to the south and he would be over his fishing grounds.

Although the old man had never set eyes on the seabed below him, it was as familiar in his minds eye as the cliffs above his village and the low water pools of the shore, where he played as a child. He knew of it, because of what his father had taught him and what he had learned, from a lifetime at sea. He knew where the reefs from the cliffs ended and mud and soft sand and broken shell began. Where sole and ray fed on worm and mollusc in the summer months and hen crabs hid in the soft ground. He knew where scallop and mussels grew and the name of every rock that fished to his advantage or threatened his boat. He knew many more things, some of which he had forgotten. Things that only a fisherman could know because nothing was written and an outsider would never be told.

Perhaps, the old man thought, he would be lucky today and catch a lobster or a fine big cock crab. It would make up for being out here, on a day like this. He had woken early that morning and considered, from the warmth of his bed, leaving the remaining pots to weather the storm. But John's passing was to close for him not to feel his brother's presence still and a sense of guilt if he did not do his best for both of them.

As the 'Mary Jane' pushed her bow beyond the point, the old man felt the strength of the swell beneath him but the waves were longer now he was free of the headland and his boat rode more easily.

To the southwest heavy seas broke on the back of Blackstone rock, framing it in white foam against the low cloud. He shook his head grimly. A touch more east in this wind, he thought and the bay will be no place to be.

"Give us an hour, wind. Just an hour." The old man implored.

"And us'll be done and out of here."

Thankfully he had only one string left to haul in open water. If he could find it quickly and the weather got no worse, he might still have time for that last pot inside the point. The thought gave him a little comfort but he cast an anxious look at the surf line on his home beach, where the swell was building.

The tide was weak and running to the north as he reached his fishing grounds. Ahead of him, the blue can buoy that marked his gear, showed between the swells. A small red flag torn and faded, flew from a bamboo pole through the buoy. The flag was visible only in the trough of the waves before the heavy seas enveloped it. The old man approached slowly letting the wind hold him off the buoy. He pushed the engine out of gear and moved forward, grasping the pole as it swung towards him and pulling it over the side to secure the rope. The 'Mary Jane' rolled and pitched on the pot line, lifting high on the swell as he prepared for the haul. The ways of the fishermen of the south coast have remained unchanged since fishing began here. Sails, have given way to motor power and natural fibre, to synthetic, for rope making and pots. But the old man still fished for crab in the time-honoured way of his kind. Weighted traps baited with fish frames and tied to a leaded line, attracted crabs and lobsters drawn by the scent of the fish. The number of pots on a line was limited only by the size of the boat and the crew's ability to handle the string. For the old man, now working alone, single pots or two on a line, were as many as he wanted.

His pots, some twenty feet apart and had been down on the seabed for several days, the first, more heavily weighted of the two, had sunk into the soft sand. Holding the boat firm, he braced his feet and freed the line as the boat dropped into a trough. He took up the slack and re-secured quickly before the bow lifted on the next swell. The old man knew well, how to use the power of the sea to his advantage and the natural buoyancy of the boat to lever the pots from the seabed. He watched carefully as the bow rose and the wet rope stretched bar taught and bit into the hard wood of the gunwhale. As the wave surged beneath him he felt the pot break free. No longer held to the seabed the 'Mary Jane' swung her bow with the wind and the old man hauled the rope as soon as they began to drift. He hauled with short straight-backed pulls and the wet line fell in coils around his feet. His hands and thigh boots ran with a brown stain of weed from the rope.

He felt the first pot strike the side of the boat and reaching into the sea, swung it up and over the gunwale. Water poured through the net-covered sides and brittle stars and broken mussel shells fell to the bottom boards, crunching beneath his boots. He rolled the pot towards the bow onto its flat base and turned at once to haul the second. Apart from the bones of the fish bait and a host of swimmer crabs, the first pot was empty. The second pot broke the surface and the old man grasped the frame and braced his knees as the boat rolled in the swell. Green water poured over the side, as he hauled it inboard and dropped it to the bottom boards. There was a large cock crab and two hens inside but the old man let them be. They were safe enough and he must attend to his boat. Quickly he moved back to the tiller, driving the bow hard across the swells towards the shelter of the headland. As he turned, a wave top struck the bow with a blow that shook every timber and covered him in spray. He cursed and shrugged the water from him, like a dog emerging from the sea. Bending low, he grasped the bilge pump lever in his right hand and pumped until the water level dropped below the bottom boards and his engine was safe.

There was now only one pot left on the shallow ground below the cliffs and the old man was reluctant to leave it. There's no harm in going in to look, he thought. If the swell is too much, I can leave it be. But he knew well enough that once there, he would get it if he could. It was in his nature.

Running the 'Mary Jane' close to the headland, he watched for the small buoy that marked his gear. He quickly found it close to the rocks, a splash of colour against a dark cave mouth. He turned his boat head to wind, to slow her and braced himself firm as the boat pitched and rolled. He felt the increasing power of the swell beneath him and watched thoughtfully as the seas broke on the headland, sweeping along the cliffs towards him. As was usual with southerly swells, the biggest of them ran in sets of three but between the sets there was usually a spell of quieter water. This was what he would need but he must have time to reach the buoy, lift the pot and get clear again before the next set reached him. The run of the waves told him there was time enough. But there was precious little time to spare. The old man pulled his hat down firmly and prepared himself, spreading his feet and bracing the tiller against his thigh. He looked around. His boat hook was to hand and his knife jammed into a frame in the stern. He was ready. For a moment he imagined his brother in the bow before him, shaking his head disapprovingly. He could hear his voice.

"You've no business out here in this sea, our Malcolm." But then he was always the cautious one, was John. It was the difference between them but it was what had made them a good crew. How he wished John was with him now, to haul, whilst he kept his boat off the rocks. The old man pushed the thought aside and straightened his back, shaking the stiffness out of his frame. His sharp eyes and all his concentration must be on the point. When the time was right, he swung the bow towards the headland and rode into the last swell of the set, as naturally, as if he and the 'Mary Jane' were one.

The boat's approach was a sweeping curve that brought her bow, head to wind alongside the buoy. Deftly he slipped the engine out of gear and gaffed up the line as he passed. He was no more than a boats length from the rocks and though he could smell the breath of the cave and the kelp weed torn by the waves, he did not look up. Low overhead herring gulls dipped and cried a warning. The boat ran on under its own weight, turning away from the cliff, as the old man had planned. Quickly, he coiled the loose line and dropped it into the bow, moving to the centre of the boat to haul. As he took the weight of the pot he felt the boat slow and her bow begin to turn back towards the rocks. She rolled on her beam, shipping green water as he hauled, splashing his thigh boots and bare arms. He shifted his weight to raise the gunwhale and balance the boat. If a wave swamped the engine, or the pot caught fast this close to the rocks, he would be for it! The rope hardened up, unyielding in his hands and the boat bucked and rolled beneath his feet. He threw the rope across his back and took the strain, glancing up anxiously at the headland. He knew he had to break it out quickly, or abandon the pot. The rope bit deep into his shoulder as the boat swung but he ignored the pain and held firm, his eyes on the point.

Seaward of Cherrick rocks, on the edge of the tide line, Ola called the seal to him through the swell and they slipped below the surface. Together they rode the tidal surge of the headland, over the kelp forest, into the deeper water of the bay. Broken weed and sediment driven by the swell, hung suspended around them and only sharp-eyed gulls saw them as they surfaced in the bay. Ola scanned the cliff line, feeling the rhythmic beat of a boat engine and quickly traced the hard outline of its floating shape. Leaving the seal on the surface, he dived and approached the boat, invisible in the clouded shallow water. The dolphin rose beneath the boat keeping his body clear of its rough surface. Held by a rope to the seabed, the hard shape lifted and crashed its bow into the sea, worrying at the rope like a trapped creature driven back and forth, by the heavy seas. Cautiously, Ola surfaced. The waves were short and spray-torn by the wind, almost submerging the craft. But as he lifted his head and the boat rolled, he saw the old fisherman towering over him, as dark and forbidding as the cliffs above. He sank back, his heart beating fast, in fear and surprise at the encounter.

Man was not an unfamiliar sight to the dolphin. He had seen the land creature many times on his journeys with the group. But it had always when the dolphins were running fast on the pressure wave of surface craft with only a glimpse of them high above the water. He had never been so close to this strange creature before. Curiosity was overcoming his surprise but he was still cautious and a little afraid. Slowly he rose again, lifting his head above the surface this time prepared for what he would see. The figure stood firm within the boat as it rolled and pitched with the violent motion of the sea. The rope that held it fast was wrapped tightly around its form. As waves broke over the dolphin's head he drove hard with his powerful tail lifting his body high out of the water in his efforts to see more clearly. Sensing, or feeling another presence, the old man turned his head and found himself confronted by the most extraordinary sight he could ever have imagined. A great dolphin rose from the broken surface of the sea beside him, close enough for him to have touched the outspread pectoral fins. The hard bottlenose lifted high above his head and the black shining body, turned slowly before him, impossibly balanced on its churning tail. For a moment their eyes met and in that moment the old man forgot the danger of his position and the pain of the pot line across his back. He could only wonder at the beauty and grace of the creature he beheld.

Ola sank slowly back into the turbulent water and the hard outline of man and boat, fragmented on the surface above him. The encounter had disturbed him. He had looked deep into the eyes of man and expected the cold dispassion of the predator shark. What he saw in that fleeting moment was fear and courage and an awareness he would only ever have associated with his own kind. The thought left him excited and confused. He rolled onto his back and dived into the forest of waving kelp, following the rope into the gloom. It twisted and chaffed among the rocks tearing kelp roots from gulley walls as the boat above, pitched in the surface swell. Deep in the rocks at the ropes end he discovered a crab pot caught fast, where the waves and the weight of the boat had driven it.

Head down in the darkness and debris of the gully, Ola held his position, mindful of the waves surge and the rock walls of sharp barnacles on either side. He slipped his hard nose under the pot and pushing up with his pectoral fins, broke it free of the gulley floor. Sand sediment and weed swirled around him as the pot tore through the kelp canopy above and into open water.

The old man felt the rope break free and the boat rear like a live thing, beneath him. This in itself might not have unbalanced him but it had come with the first of the big swells and as the bow lifted, high into the air, he lost his footing and fell forwards into the boat. He fell heavily onto his knees on the thin wooden frames, clinging to the thwart with both hands, the rope discarded. Face down on the hard seat he struggled to get his breath, trying to ignore the pain in his chest and knees. Reaching forward he pushed the engine into gear and twisted round to catch the swinging tiller and control the boat. It was impossible to hear his engine above the breaking seas but the old man could feel the throb of power through the tiller bar and the boat responding. He lifted his head, forcing himself up from his knees. The cliff face rose like a lift, streaming water from the swell, black and forbidding before him. The old man cursed aloud and in a fury of desperation, snatched up an oar and grasping it in both hands drove it hard into the cliff face. Limpets and kelp weed tore and shattered on the rock under the onslaught but the stout wood held and pushing with all his strength he held the 'Mary Jane' clear of the rocks.

The old man had only the strength to hold her for a moment but it was enough. He felt the new swell run beneath him like fresh blood through his veins. His boat lifted at the stern, the screw biting deep into the cushion of water and slowly the 'Mary Jane' pulled herself to safety. The pot trailed in the surface foam of the boats wake as the Mary Jane's speed increased. He closed the throttle, his hands shaking with strain and with his remaining strength he gathered in the rope and pulled the pot alongside. The gunwale dipped under his weight as he grasped the frame and the boat pitched heavily in the swell. Rolling the pot up and over the side into the boat the old man left it where it lay and collapsed heavily onto the seat. He had the taste of blood on his bruised lips mingling with the salt spray and his limbs trembled with fatigue. He could seldom remember feeling so tired and he was stiff and cold and he felt something else too. It was a sudden doubt, in his strength and his own ability to cope out here any more.

The very thought galvanised the old man into action and he pushed himself painfully to his feet, brushing the thought aside. Anyone could have been unnerved by the sight of that dolphin and lost their footing in the swell. And hadn't he stood his ground and torn that pot out and got clear. Was that the action of an old man who could no longer read the sea or handle his boat. He shook his head, turning his face to the open sea defiantly. But the thought was planted in his mind and he felt the weaker for it. He must get back to the village as quickly as he could, for the weather was worsening and there was little time to get the 'Mary Jane' safely ashore.

The old man looked anxiously over his shoulder as the swells built behind him and the wind blew white streaked spray across his back. He grasped the tiller firm and braced his feet. The swell was building and turning east with the wind and the tops were breaking. He thought. It will be a big sea at the beach, when I get back but we have landed in worse than this, John and me. Didn't they always say that we could fish when no others would put to sea? That the two of us could land a 'dry boat' in an easterly gale!

"And it is the truth". Malcolm shouted aloud. "It's the truth"

He banged his clenched fist on the tiller bar and lifted a defiant face to the dark sky. Ahead of him beyond the rolling swell, white surf broke on the rocks of the old village. As the old man neared the shore, he stood up once more, flexing his limbs against the pain in his shoulders and knees. He remembered his oilskin top beneath the seat and dragged it out slipping it over his head. He held the tiller between his legs, to pull the cover down over his waders. The wind was strengthening all the time, chilling his damp clothes and he could feel his joints stiffening with cold. I must stay sharp and keep my wits about me to land the boat, he thought. And he nodded grimly and kept the thought in his mind. Approaching the shore with deep water still beneath him, the old man swung his bow seaward, into the swells. He looked back at the beach, pulling his cap down for security against the wind, eyes narrowed, watching the big waves breaking. It was only half tide but he saw that already the sea was reaching the high water mark. He knew he must beach the boat soon, or the swell would make a safe landing impossible. He circled, running in as close as he dared to judge the pattern of the waves, watching with care as the big sets ran beneath him. If he were caught at the beach by a big swell it would swamp him! He turned on a wave top and faced the shore, waiting for his moment. His plan was a simple one and depended for its success on his experience and understanding of the sea. He would use the energy of the waves to ride the crest of a swell all the way to the shore, driving onto the beach at full power, as close to the winch wire as possible. The impact would stop the 'Mary Jane' in her tracks despite her speed but if he could land stern on to the seas, the next swell, could push his boat to safety up the beach. The old man knew that timing was everything and he must not think of what might happen if he got it wrong... He had done this many times before with his brother. Now he must have the faith to do it alone!

The wind had backed more into the east and spray from the swells breaking on the bow, was driving the length of the boat, lashing the old man's hands and face and pooling in the oilskin of his lap. He wiped the salt from his eyes to see the pattern of the waves, as he had off the point and despite the spray and breaking tops, could clearly see their run on the cliff line. The old man chose his moment with care, turning towards the shore and taking a sight on the winch over the bow. He must land close enough to be able to quickly attach the wire to the boat. He looked back, watching the speed of the approaching swells and opened the throttle of the engine. The first lifted the boat and ran its length, dropping her stern first, into the following trough. He judged its speed, as it ran on to the shore and opened the throttle. He must be close to the speed of the next wave, if it was to support him. The second came, bigger than the first and he felt the bow drop before him as the wave lifted the "Mary Jane" and carried her forward. The motor raced as the speed increased and he knew then he was committed. He was on the face of the wave. There would be no more waiting and no going back.

The old man braced himself clutching the tiller with both hands. White knuckles on the dark wood, as the "Mary Jane" creamed towards the shore. The sea roared beneath him and spray covered his boat obscuring the land but he kept her straight and he could feel only the excitement of the moment and the adrenalin pumping through his veins like the blood of his youth. "Come on me beauty... Come on". He cried aloud. Clutching the tiller with both hands and willing the boat to stay on the wave top till the end.

"Yes! Yes!" He shouted again, triumphantly, as the boat ploughed onto the beach and the last of the wave thundered onto the shingle ridge. He jumped ashore struggling, knee deep in water and sliding shingle. As the wave receded, he saw the rusty winch wire at his feet. Careless of his bruises, he dropped to his hands and knees and grabbed for the hook. Behind him he heard the thunder of the next swell breaking. A moment before the weight of water struck, the old man threw himself forward and snapped the hook onto the brass ring in the bow. The force of the impact of the wave drove the bow past him and half a boats length further up the beach. He dug his feet and fingers deep into the shingle as the water receded swirling around him and threatening to pull him back into the sea. As soon as he was able he reached up, clutching the side of the boat and pulling himself erect. But there was no time to rest, he must secure the boat. Wearily the old man forced himself to climb the beach to the pulley block and drag the slack of the rusting wire through the metal sheath. A tapered hardwood wedge driven home with a heavy stone secured the sheath and as the swell receded under the stern of the 'Mary Jane the winch wire tightened and held her fast. At sea, Ola turned his back on the headland and Cherrick rocks. His small bay now swamped in white water with curtains of spray reaching the lower ledges. Roosting birds were driven into the air, their cries lost in the wind and thunder of the surf. Ola rode tail down into the wind and heavy swell, shepherding the seal in close beside him. For the sake of his young companion he must leave and find shelter from the heavy seas.

A dark unbroken line of cliffs stretched ahead of them and black storm clouds, chased by the wind, lay at their backs. The water of Ola's hunting grounds darkened with debris and sand, lifted from the seabed, Shadows of wrasse and shoal fish heeding the warning, fled beneath them for the rocks and caves of deeper water.

On the surface of the open sea Ola quickly found they were in the grip of the storm. Water and sky became one and the wind joined in song with the thunder of the sea and lifted the swell high above them. Lashed with foam, that filled the very air they breathed, the two creatures twisted and surfed through the breaking crests as the storm drove them on. Ola would have dived for much of the journey, into the calm of mid water but for his fear of loosing the seal. The tiny creature was finding it increasingly difficult to keep up. It would cling tired and dejected to his fins at every opportunity, gasping for air as the seas broke over them.

Scanning ahead for the shelter they so desperately needed, Ola traced a headland stretching before them into the sea. The storm drove them on and the waves increased in height as they approached the end of the cliff line. Beyond it they would find the protection they needed. As they approached, Ola saw a great rock standing high out of the water, close to the headland, spotted with circling gulls. All around its foot the waves foamed white, as the sea broke on the shallow ground. Great reefs of rock showed between the swells, spreading like kelp roots from the base, far out to sea.

Ola felt a new unrest, as they neared the headland. A force that clutched and pulled in all directions as storm waves met the tidal forces of the point of land. His heart quickened and Ola anxiously scanned the turbulent shallows ahead for a way through the reef. At the last moment with the swells breaking to foam all around them, Ola turned and dived towards the shore, with the seal close behind him. At the foot of the big rock, he found what he was looking for. It was a narrow channel of clear water between the reef and the land. Kelp fronds on the gulley floor streamed flat beneath them as they slipped between walls of rock. In a moment they were through, into the calm sheltered water on the far side of the point.

Ola surfaced, venting his lungs with relief in the clear air. He looked anxiously around. A small head broke the surface beside him and big eyes looked into his. With a cry of excitement the seal rolled on its back before him, its tiredness forgotten. Clutched to its chest it proudly displayed a plump fish, which it at once began to eat. Ola sighed resentfully and flexed his aching body, dipping his head into a wave top and shaking water over his back. He was very tired and wanted only to rest in the quiet water until daylight. The storm behind the headland seemed thankfully far away.

When Ola woke the storm was still raging but there was no sign of his companion. He swam towards the channel that had been their passage the previous day. Rolling seas shrouded the headland with a mist of flying spray as they thundered onto the rocks. Above him, gulls called to one another their cries lost in the high wind. The dolphin did not resist the current that pushed him back into the quiet water knowing the seal would not have come this way. But where was he? Hiding his anxiety he turned away and swam to the west, leaving the high rocks of the point behind him.

This new territory was not unlike the area Ola had left. The high cliffs continued but at their foot the rock was flawed with caves and groins running deep into the cliffs. Wet rock exposed by the tide, glistened in the dark mouths of the caves. It was seal country and not surprising he had lost his companion. A gull screamed a warning as Ola turned towards the shore and he saw dark shapes separate from the rocks at the waters edge and move towards the cliffs. Two females were leading a group of young seals back to the caves, calling them with anxious cries.   Ola lifted his head but it was too far to see if one of them was his young charge. On an outcrop of rock a large bull seal lay motionless, his head turned towards the dolphin. Ola moved closer, letting his body sink, only the tip of his dorsal fin cut the surface. As the water shallowed a wall of rock topped with weed at the surface, appeared before him. He could go no further. Letting his tail sink Ola again lifted his head. He was close enough now to see that several of the caves were occupied but no seals were left out on the rocks. Suddenly a small movement caught his eye close to where the bull seal lay. A tiny head lifted above the weed and a young seal emerged. Clutched awkwardly in its claws was a struggling fish. The dolphin was in no doubt that he had found his seal. The bull lifted its head teeth bared and bellowed a warning, fixing Ola with a baleful stare. The baby seal was suddenly aware of the presence of the dolphin and lifted itself high on its flippers, calling in his direction. Ola hit the surface with his fin. Making it clear the seal should stay where it was. But he called reassuringly. He knew it was time for him to go and leave the seal with its own kind. His presence would only alarm the group further and he had no wish to do battle with the bull seal.

The dolphin filled his lungs with air and turned away, slipping quietly below the surface. He was not really sorry to be free of his young charge. He had wearied of its dependency and now slow, in his movements and abilities, he would have been further restricted by the small creature, had it stayed. He swam low over a shelving sandy bottom and scattered rocks to a cliff edge and the deep water beyond. The velvet darkness of the deep was a welcome embrace, but the distant signal from the soft ocean floor only heightened his feeling of isolation.

He felt a renewed longing for the companionship of one of his own kind and his heart ached for the return of his group. But with the feeling of loneliness, came the thought. Surely there must be others like him. Dolphins, forced to leave their group, who had adapted and survived, just as he had. He could not be the only one.

He vented his lungs and let the darkness embrace him as he sank slowly towards the ocean floor. The thought that he might find others, filled him with new hope and purpose and he turned his head to the north and began to swim. He would return to his cove in the shallows and the fishing grounds of man and if there were others of his kind, he would find them

Chapter Four

The old fisherman drifted towards consciousness from his dreams of summers at sea with his brother John and a gentle wind in the sail pushing them home. Away from a sea quiet and still, as it always was in his dreams and a sky as blue as the ocean depths. He steered a boat with a patched and faded sail and the timbers were bare and worn. But his hand on the tiller was a young man's hand and his brother moved before him with all the tireless strength of youth. On the bottom boards, at his feet, a fine catch of fish lay; smooth dark shapes, under cool wet sacking.

The cottage was dark when he woke but there was light under his door, warm with the rising sun. He lay still on his iron bed against the wall and listened to the restless sounds of the house. For a moment, his waking thoughts were still with his brother and the dry rustle of bramble and gorse, against the outside wall, brought back half forgotten memories of their childhood.

The back of the house was cut deep into the cliff, so close that only a small child might crawl between the soft earth and the stone. It had been their secret place, as boys and he and John had brought drift wood from the shore and tarred rope and blocks from the wrecks of ships and when bad weather drove them from the beach they would crawl behind the cottage, shut out the wind and sail the world through the storms of winter...

The old man smiled. It pleased him to think that everything would still be there just as they had left it. A child's world locked in time in a place that only another small child might find, or understand.

He pushed himself erect, his joints, stiff and painful and swung his feet to the cool linoleum floor. Although he had rested well, it had been two days since he had been caught out in the bad weather, his whole body still ached from his fall at sea and his struggle to bring the 'Mary Jane' ashore.

Thoughts of his ordeal pushed childhood memories aside and he shook his head, lifting a hand to knead the stiff tendons of his neck. He should never have gone for that last pot. That was a mistake, he thought. In his minds eye, he could see his brothers' grim smile and nod of agreement.

"But I got her back, didn't I." He said, defensively. "That's what counts"

But he knew how close he had been to loosing his boat and the feeling of not being able to cope out there, had not left him. Nor had the despair of winching his boat to the block and turning to find waves reaching the cliffs like a winter storm. With little left but his determination, he had climbed down to free his boat from the block and save her being dashed against the cliffs. The water had risen to his waist and lifted the stern of the 'Mary Jane' but he had held her, setting himself hard against the gunwale and swinging the boat as she floated until the bow lined up with the cliff path. He had told himself he could have held her steady for a second wave, if he had to. But he had prayed in his heart that he would not be put to the test. Fortunately she had settled into the shingle as the wave retreated, giving him time to scramble to the winch and pulled her to safety. The effort had cost him dear and he had taken to his bed and slept through the height of the storm and most of the following day.

It is said that a fisherman will always know when it is time to come ashore and lay up his boat and in his heart the old man knew this to be right and his time was near. But calm seas had quickly returned to the bay with a promise of fine weather and the old man had pushed his doubts aside. He thought, John would never expect him to quit if the fish could be easily caught. The old man shook his head and managed a thin smile. He knew the good weather was all the excuse he needed to stay afloat. But he would take it easy and fish within the reaches of the bay and when the weather looked like breaking then he would stop. He sat for a moment longer before pulling his crumpled clothes from the foot of the bed. He would have a bowl of soup and a cup of tea to give him strength and he would be ready to get the 'Mary Jane' back on to the beach.

The old man dropped his mooring buoy from the bow and moved to the stern of his boat, pushing the engine into gear, before the tide could take it seaward. It was late afternoon, there was no wind and a sea mist hung like smoke on the rocks of the headland. He lifted his cap and settled it more securely and cast an approving eye over his boat. He had spent the morning preparing her and he was well pleased with his efforts. She was pumped out and clean, smelling of fresh fish and pine wood, the way a work boat should and there was not a brittle star or piece of broken shell to be seen. The fresh painted for-peak deck shone bright and wet salt crystals sparkled in the sunlight. He had done a proper job for his last day at sea and the old man felt that his brother would have approved.

He looked down into the empty boat before him. At the sweep of the boards and the damaged floor where the trays of bait and pots had been and the rope-cuts across timber as worn as his hands from a lifetime of hauling and he thought of his brother and their life together and for a moment, of the bad times and there were plenty of those if he chose to remember.... But he would not think of them today. A thin smile creased his weathered face. Today, he would think only of the good times when the two of them were working together and the fish were running and the summers days were as warm as this.

Besides, there was little comfort in bad memories for an old man.

"A lifetime, we have been out here, you and me John." He said aloud and shook his head.

"A lifetime... It don't seem possible but it's the truth." And not much to show for it neither, he thought. Not in the way folks have today.

"But we caught some fish, didn't we John. That's for sure, there weren't a boat could better us."

The old man nodded with satisfaction and a smile. He dropped his head in reflection, balancing easily to the movement of his boat on the gentle swell. Gulls called over the cliffs and the water slopped hollow under the stern. The exhaust popped and spluttered as it dipped below the water and he felt through his boots the rhythmic beat of the engine like the heart of his boat. He thought it a rare day to be at sea and he was content.

A diving bird broke the surface, close by shaking water from its wings and he turned towards the sound. The shag lifted its body high on the surface and shook its wings free of water, smoothing its dark feathers, emerald green in the sunlight. It held a large sand eel in its sharp beak, shaking its head to turn the fish and swallow it whole. The eel bulged grotesquely in its thin neck and the old man always marveled, at the ability of these birds to eat there prey whole. He had seen them trying to swallow flatfish and take five minutes to get them down, gagging with the effort. The bird dipped its head and drank to ease the passage of the eel then raised its feathered crest and fixed him with a hard stare.

The old man leant forward and closed the throttle lever down. The engine revolutions dropped to tick over, just keeping the boat alive, with enough way on to hold steerage in the tide. There was not a breath of wind and but for the slight swell the sea was as flat as a dab. He marveled at the tranquility of it all, he always did on a day like this. And he had only to sail to the point, spread the ashes of his brother and go home and beach his boat. It was a strange feeling to come to sea and do no fishing.

He felt the tide strengthen beneath him as he moved away, the high cliffs of the headland slipping slowly past like a tapestry of his whole life. He shielded his eyes with his hand, scanning the coastline. He could see his cottage above the village where he was born and the narrow cliff path down to the ruins and the rock pools and gulleys where he and John had laid their first pots.

He turned the flat of his hand to obscure the lower cliffs, leaving only his cottage and the sweep of the headland in view. Everything now was as it had always been and he was transported in a moment, to a silver shingle beach with the old village sharp in the sunlight. The old man sighed and dropped his hand, shaking his head. It was becoming more and more difficult relating that picture to what remained. In a couple of years, he thought, there would be nothing left, to show the village had ever been.

As the thought struck home, he was reminded of how significant this day was. Not only his brother's last day on their fishing grounds but his own. It was the end of a life at sea for both of them and marked the end of a community that had lasted three hundred years. Suddenly the old man felt a closeness to his brother he had seldom felt before and a need to prolong this last day and share some memories and somehow make their time together last a little longer.

He turned the bow of 'The Mary Jane' back towards the cliffs shifting his feet to balance, as he opened the throttle. The shag surfaced ahead of him, beating the water with a loud slapping of its broad wet wings as it took off into the sunlight.

Dark rocks showed beneath the surface as the Mary Jane neared the shore, slipping out of the sunlight into the shadow of the cliff. The sea was as quiet as a pool and there was no swell at the waters edge. Nesting kittiwakes spotting the rocks above the ruins, covered their chicks and called anxiously to each other at the boat drew near. The shag had landed on a rocky ledge in a shaft of sunlight, its wings outspread like an apron drying in the breeze.

The old man cut the motor of the 'Mary Jane' and drifted towards a rock rising high out of the narrow beach. He knew it well and he and his brother had played around it as children, when only its top, a small nub of rock had shown above the shingle. Now with the beach gone, it towered over him, like a monument, dominating the ruins. The old man lifted an oar and held himself off the rock balancing easily on the quiet sea. The ruins lay before him, desolate in the shadow of the cliff. Broken walls on flimsy archways of crumbling rock spanned the narrow beach and the water swirled shingle restlessly, in the caves and groins between.

He looked up, above the kittiwakes nests to the cliff top where a low stone wall showed through the gorse. It marked the old road down to the village and he tracked its path to the Prettyjohn's cottage where his friend Lissie Ann had spent her life. She was as brave as any that had endured the storms and the last to leave, refusing to budge whilst she had walls around her and breath in her body. And she was as good as her word, thought the old man with a smile.

He stared reflectively for a moment at the empty cottage, with its salt scoured stone and dead shuttered eyes. Its high position had saved it from the sea and it had been bought up quickly enough when Lizzie died but it was not a real home any more, not as he saw it anyway. Just a holiday cottage for occasional visitors who couldn`t know what had gone before and wouldn`t be here when the sea was up and an easterly was tearing the heart out of what was left. Beyond the cottage, the path abruptly ended at a fall of rock, into a deep crevasse.

Of the houses that had stood here there was no sign. All that remained was a line of joist pockets in the smooth rock face that had once formed the back walls of the cottages. The old man stared intently at the broken shelf of rock, trying to get his bearings. The London Inn would have been over the archway to his left with Stone's cottage behind it and the shop up a ways. The old man pushed back his cap and scratched his head, frowning in thought. That would put Login's house above him over to the right and the boat slip beyond. And he could still see 'Long rock' at the southern end of the village where the Trout's house had been.

The old man shook his head, driving the oar against the rock and pushing the boat into the warm sunlight. The water beneath him was clear but dark with weed, where kelp fronds clung to broken fragments of the old sea wall. He sat down and bent low over the gunwhale close to the water, cupping his hands to shield his eyes. There was little he could recognize. Erosion and marine growth had softened the concrete structures, rock like in their disguise and only when he spied a run of wall protruding from the seabed free of growth, could he be sure of what he had found. Scoured and pitted by the action of the sea he made out the domed top of the old boat slip wall.

"Well bless me John." The old man said.

"It's where us sat as kids to watch for the boats. Where the reporter took our photo. You and me and Cyril Stone... and John Login."

The old man glanced around and straightened up, facing the empty boat. He grinned self-consciously and sat for a moment elbows on his knees; remembering four small boys playing in the dust of the village street in the late afternoon sunshine. Chasing chickens they were and the willow sticks they beat in the dust would be put across their backsides if they were caught. A tall stranger had appeared and a bag of boiled sweets had persuaded them to sit together and have their photograph taken. As children, it had meant nothing to them at the time but everyone was well pleased to see it printed in the local newspaper with an article on the plight of the village. It was one of many articles in the struggle to save the village, the old man reflected. But it all came to naught, in the end. He rose to his feet and dropping the oars into the rowlocks began to steer the boat stern first with the tide.

Beyond 'Long rock' narrow fingers of rock ran eastwards over the white sand into deep water. Here, the coastline had suffered less from the dredging and the old man could pick out familiar spots where he had crab fished as a boy. It was where his grandfather William, had taught him and John much of their trade, whilst they was still too young to go to sea. He remembered. They would spend hours among the rocks, awash at the low water mark, hunting fine cock crabs in holes only a foot or so beneath the kelp weed. The cocks were after the soft hen crabs they were but you had to know where to find them.

On impulse the old man moved to the bow, dropping oars into the forward rowlocks and pulling the boat back towards 'Long rock'.

"Let's see what's about, whilst we're here, shall us." He said aloud.

He grinned, feeling a twinge of anticipation at the thought of what was to come. Hunting for crab in the shallows was never worth breaking into a days potting for or missing a tide. But it was rare fun on a quiet day with time on your hands. John would understand.

The reef was awash at its seaward end with a skirt of weed floating around its edge and dark shadows of rock below. The old man brought the boat close and shipped oars. He lifted a small anchor tied at the bow and before the boat could move back with the tide, threw it up onto the rock. Satisfied that it held him secure, he tied off the rope at around thirty feet and with the slack coiled in his hand, he stepped carefully ashore.

The Mary Jane slipped back with the tide as the old man eased out the slack of the rope, until she lay clear of the rocks. He knew the tide would not let him spend much time on the reef and he could not move far from his boat but there were pits and crevasses below where he stood, that with luck should fish well enough.

Hitching the folds out of his waders and holding firmly to the anchored rope for support the old man dipped one foot into the floating kelp, feeling for a ledge below the surface. He was knee deep before he found it and had to grip the rough surface of the rock with his hands to keep his balance but he grunted with satisfaction. His memory hadn't failed him. He pulled on the rope shifted his weight to bring down the other foot and stood erect, facing the rock. Now all he had to do was work his way seaward along the ledge feeling with his boots for the crabs. The ledge was only about ten feet long and sloping down towards the seabed but with luck he could reach the end and stay dry.

He moved slowly keeping the slack out of the rope exploring the ledge with his right foot, all the while watching for a swell that might catch him out and flood his boots. He felt a crab, like a flat stone struggle beneath his boot for a moment and lifted his weight to release it. It was too small. Two more cavities at the back of the ledge produced nothing and the old man was nearly at the end, with water half way up his thighs, before he found what he was looking for.

He felt the broad back of a large crab shift beneath him. Pushing down with his foot he prevented its escape but big crabs were strong and thrusting up with its legs, it trapped his foot in the narrow space above.

He knew he could lever his foot free and escape but then he would loose the crab and the old man had no intention of doing that. Dropping the rope for a moment he pulled his sweater over his head, tossing it with his cap up on the rock clear of the water and rolling his shirt sleeves high up his muscular arms. Clutching the rope again and pulling it taught he bent at the waist, sliding his hand down the side of his wader and under the heel. His face was barely inches from the water and his breath broke the surface wetting his cheeks. He grunted with satisfaction as he felt the bulge of a large claw protruding from the side of his boot. Dragging his foot free he grabbed the side of the claw as the crab lifted to attack and tore it from the ledge, sweeping it up through the surface, spraying his shirt front with water.

"Got you, me beauty" He shouted aloud.

He dropped the rope over his arm and grasped its rearmost legs before it could attack him with the other claw. In a moment it was his. The old man grinned with delight, lifting it high and waving it in triumph towards the boat. It was fine crab, around eight pounds he judged and well worth the time and effort.

The old man slipped a bight of rope over the shell and tightened it above the legs so it could not escape and scrambled stiffly onto the rock

He straightened his back pulling a face with the effort, waiting for the trembling in his legs to stop. It was a curse this stiffening up but it always happened if he held a position to long. The old man shrugged off his discomfort as best he could he knew he should not complain, he was in better shape than most. He slipped on his sweater and cap and hauled his boat back to the rocks. He was aboard in a moment and drifting clear with the engine running and his catch tucked into a wet sack in the bow. The old man was well pleased with himself.

"We are still up to it John. Still know where to find em." He said.

Beyond the village and the shallow reefs and rock groins the cliff line rose and strengthened, curving towards the south and the great cockscombe shoulder of Start Point. In the early spring and summer the headland was ablaze with colour and even now where sheep grazed above the old mans head on the cliff tops, bluebells still showed amongst the course grasses.

The old man turned once again towards the shore as the water deepened under him, running close in at the highest part of the cliff. Roosting gulls lifted and circled restlessly screaming a warning to each other, with the bravest of them diving on the boat to drive him away. The old man put the boat out of gear and floated in, looking up at the face of Gull rock rising fifty feet above him to the nesting ledges. He braced his knee against the gunwale and reached out to touch the rough stone surface. He fancied he could still see where small feet had scrabbled for a grip on the cliff face, as two eager youngsters raced each other to the nesting ledges. He looked up as more and more gulls lifted from the rock and joined the flock circling uneasily above him.

"Ah, You remember us, birds. " He said aloud.

And you have good reason to, he thought. But you have nothing to fear now, that's for sure. Couldn`t climb up there now if I wanted. Mind you, there was a time when we would have had one from every nest without them missing an egg. And get 3d each for them…Thought we were millionaires we did. The old man chuckled at the memory and pushed his boat away from the cliff face.

He slipped the engine into gear, watching cautiously for the weed-covered rocks below the surface. As he moved, eel shoals, swept dark lines across the sand patches and flashed silver in the sunlight ahead of him. Kelp weed, trailed fronds on the still surface and in the distance the lighthouse sounded a mournful note of warning.

The old man lifted his head towards the sound. The crown of the lighthouse showed, floating above the low mist and a tail of fog stretched from it out to sea but there was still no wind and nothing was moving. He watched for a moment until he was satisfied the fog was not thickening before moving on.

Beyond Gull rock, the dark arch of a cave appeared, barely showing above the tide line. The old man knew that its narrow mouth concealed a large chamber within the cliff, rising from water level and running far back, high and dry, into the headland. It was a birth cave for Atlantic seals and only the local fishermen knew of it.

The old man slowed the engine for a moment and lifted his head, listening and sniffing the air like a hound. But there was no stale smell of fish or slap of a fin to betray the presence of a seal. Give them a couple of months, he thought and they will be dropping their pups in the back there, where the storms can't get them, snug as you like.... Nature is a wonderful thing.

"But us could reach em." He said with a smile. "Couldn't us John."

He thought. We would go in at low tide and crawl all the way up to see em...Suckling pups as fat as barrels...tumbled on top of each other and smelling like a fish market.... It's the truth. And what about the time that bull seal nearly had you John. Came down the tunnel like a train, he did... He was after you for sure. Bellowing and snapping. Never saw you move so fast in all me life.

"Up the wall like a monkey you were." He said aloud, with a chuckle. Still smiling to himself the old man motored seaward following the cliff line at a safe distance towards the point. At its outermost limit, before the lighthouse, a stone wall followed the ridge to the cliff edge. It was here, high above the water of the bay, his brother would sit and watch for the fish shoals.

There was no one on this coast could spot fish like our John, the old man thought proudly. Eyes like a hawk he had. And he knew when they were going to be there.

"A rare gift that is" He said aloud

This was a fitting place right enough, to spread his ashes.

A small red buoy trailed a ripple of tide on the smooth water ahead of him and the old man pushed the engine out of gear and picked up the float as it brushed the side of the boat. He tied it off at the bow and switched off the engine and moving back to sit down heavily in the stern. In the quiet that followed the tide sang its melody around the boat and fingers of mist began to creep across the water, as if to hide the old man from prying eyes.

He reached below the seat and carefully lifted up a small pewter casket, cradling it between his knees, its elegant shape lost in his large work torn hands. The soft sunlight through the mist sparkled on the cap and the old man ran a knarled finger around the seam of the lid. He felt the beating of his heart as he held it and for a moment he hesitated, as if unsure of what he should do; what was expected of him.

He thought of the pact he and his brother had made as children. When they had promised that whoever was left would bury the other at sea; out on the fishing grounds that meant so much to them both. The promise had come easily and the solemn moment made light with laughter, when they couldn't agree where the place should be. The old man smiled sadly.

We always argued about everything, he thought. But it didn't matter... All brothers do that.

"It didn't mean nothing," he said. He looked up again, to John's mark on the cliffs.

"There was never a time we didn't look out for each other."

The old man shielded his eyes, peering through the mist, fancying that the dark shadow by the wall might be something more solid. "That you up there now, our John. Can't see like I used to...Tucked in out of the wind... With a flagon of cider at your feet...I wouldn't put it past you."

He grinned. His brother thought no one knew about his drinking. He would keep it in that old sail bag so nobody ever saw him at it. But that bag was always a good deal lighter when he came down from the point. The old man wanted to laugh but the chuckle caught fast in his throat.

" Best get it done, like I promised." He said aloud.

He thought. The funeral people would have done it for us, out of Dartmouth. But you wouldn't have wanted no strangers, fussing around. I know that. He loosened the lid, his fingers, shaking a little. When, a thought struck him. He would haul the pot he was tied to first, John was always the lucky one.

"If there be a lobster to go with the crab, it will be one apiece." He said.

The old man grinned, relief showing on his face as he put the casket carefully down, wedging it against the transom in the stern. Swinging the engine into life, he moved to the bow and took hold of the pot rope pulling it back to the middle of the boat. Bracing his knees against the planking he began to haul, dropping the rope into loops on the bottom boards beside him.

It was an easy haul and the heavy single pot quickly came free of the rocky bottom. Slowly the boat drifted seaward and the old man continued to haul with an unbroken rhythm until he felt the thump of the pot against the boat side. Keeping the tension on the rope with one hand he reached down and grasped the pot frame, bracing himself for the snatch lift that would bring it up on to the edge of the boat.

As the gunwhale dipped under the load the old man remembered the casket and looked up quickly towards the stern. To his dismay he saw it fall and roll across the seat. The thought of it spilling its contents into his boat drove all other thoughts from his mind. He let the pot go and kicking the heavy loops of rope away from his feet, lunged towards the stern in a desperate attempt to catch the casket as it fell. But the boat was small and the old man no agile youngster. Tangled loops of rope tightened around his legs and in a moment he felt the weight of the pot. All thoughts of the casket were forgotten, as he twisted around and tried to take the weight off the rope and loosen the bight around his legs. But the pot reached the seabed and caught fast, swinging the boat across the tide and dragging the old man into the water. Desperately he clung to the gunwale, with both hands. He knew at once he was in terrible danger. With all the strength he could muster, he threw an arm into the boat clamping it painfully to the timbers in a vice like grip. Head and shoulders above the water, he strained in an agony of effort, to pull himself back into the boat but he could not.

He lifted his face to the sky and cried aloud through clenched teeth.

"I won't go. I won't,"

He locked his jaw down on the gunwale to spread the load, his teeth bared against the pain and cast frantic eyes around the boat for anything he might reach that would help him. But there was nothing...except. Suddenly he saw one chance. A rope end attached at the bow lay on the bottom boards...If he could reach it and wind it round his body. With no more strength or time to think the old man reached into the boat, clawed up the rope and threw a loop around one shoulder. He managed a turn on the rope end across his chest before his grip was torn from the boat and he was dragged below the surface. His one thought as he was pulled down was to hold on to his lifeline at all cost and he hauled on it with both hands and all his strength. The rope dug deep into the flesh of his back and chest and the weight of the pot stretched every sinew in his body. If he let go, he would drown but he would not think of it. The surface and the sunlight was scarcely a hands breath above his head. Through the green mist of water above his white swollen hands he could see the dark shadow of the boat swinging across the tide above him. If he could shorten the rope by only a foot, he could reach it.

All at once he felt the pressure ease on his trapped legs as the pot moved on the seabed below him. Pulling with all his strength he dragged himself to the surface, striking his head hard against the hull but he felt nothing of the pain and scrabbled blindly for a grip on the rough timber. Coughing and retching salt water from his lungs, he grasped the edge of the gunwale and pulled himself up, holding his head for a precious moment above the water. Almost at once he felt the grip of the coils again and in his minds eye saw the pot-digging deep into the hard rocks below him. His chance was gone.

Fighting for his life he thrust the rope end through the eye in the bow and knotted it as best he could. As the pot line tightened it dragged his body back into the water, tearing his fingers from their hold. His face was ground against the boat, his shoulders crushed and twisted by the loop around him but his knot held and he sank no further. The old man began to shake convulsively feeling his senses reel and consciousness slipping from him. He was afraid for his life but he had been afraid before and he must put the fear to the back of his mind, as he always did. He knew that it was only despair not fear that would destroy him.

Gasping for air he slowly recovered his breath and brought the shaking under control, struggling to clear his mind and think of a way to save himself. The fog had thickened into misted clouds around him and if he shouted for help it would muffle his cries and the effort weaken him further. Anyway, he was now too far from the land to be heard. He felt the temperature drop as the fog covered the sun and he shivered, feeling the cold chill of the water for the first time. He must keep moving. His arms were free, though restricted by the loop that held him and he braced one arm against the boat to protect his face, groping beneath the water in an effort to free himself.

The pot line had caught him at the waist and wound around his thigh boots, driving the heavy rubber into his flesh. While the pressure of the tide held him, escape seemed impossible. Somehow he must hold on until it slackened. But he was so low in the water, if any wind brought waves before the tide turned, he would drown on the surface. It will be an hour or perhaps an hour and a half before slack tide. He thought. But I can hold on till then if I have to.

He pulled his elbows in together to reduce the flow of water around his body, thankful for the woolen sweater beneath his smock. He must conserve his body warmth as best he could. He would need all his strength when the time came. Suddenly, he remembered the knife. Everything had happened so quickly, there had been no time to think of it. He had a penknife in the back pocket of his jeans. It was a small folding knife but strong and sharp enough to cut through the ropes that bound him. If only he could reach it. Please God the ropes did not prevent him.

His heart pounded with excitement and relief at the thought his ordeal might soon be over and he struggled to reach back underwater feeling for the hard outline of the knife. With numbed trembling fingers he carefully drew it from his pocket and lifted it to his face where he could see it, dragging open the blade with his teeth and hearing the click of the spring as it was set. He closed his eyes for a moment and pressed the blade to his swollen lips. The foghorn sounded its mournful bellow but to the old man it was a cry of triumph as he began to saw at his bonds.

He reached as low as he could, fearful that his legs might still be held if he cut to high, pushing in the point of the knife and cutting away from his body. The blade was sharp and the rope severed quickly but he felt an agony of pain as blood returned to his lower limbs. Loose coils floated to the surface around him but to his horror he found it was not enough to free him. His feet were still held fast and he could reach no lower.

The old man was on the edge of despair and drove the knife deep into the wood above his head collapsing against the boat side. His strength was gone and he felt a renewed tiredness that was overwhelming and a desperate need for the cold and the pain to stop.

He dropped his head and closed his eyes, his senses swimming. Childhood memories played before him. He saw the image of two young boys on a beach in the sunshine. One was struggling to launch a boat. His small feet digging deep into the shingle, his arms straining in a vain attempt to move it. The other standing by and teasing his companion for his lack of strength. He heard his brothers mocking voice.

"Well that's it then Malcolm, is it... Giving up are we."

The old man lifted his head and opened his eyes. The knife blade shone wet in the mist above him. No he was not done. Not yet. There was a way; a last desperate way. Deliberately he reached up and pulled the knife from the wood and with one sweeping movement across the loop that held him, cut himself free of the Mary Jane.

At once the tide drew him down and the water closed over his head. Salt water blinded him and he could see only the shape of his white hands in the darkness. The water pressure pounded in his ears but he felt for the end of the coil he had severed and grasping it in both hands, pulled himself down to the rope that held him. His head swam and his lungs were bursting with the effort but in the dark of mid water, he felt the pot rope in his hand and with one desperate stroke cut it through. He was free!

Kicking the coils from his boots he lifted his arms and struggled weakly towards the surface. The one thought in his exhausted mind was a prayer that he could reach his boat. His sodden clothes and heavy boots pulled him down and it seemed an age before the water lightened above him and he thrust his head into the air. He lay still for a moment on the surface, head back mouth gapping, in an agony of convulsions as he tried to breath. Mercifully, the Mary Jane lay only feet away in the mist and he struggled to her side and grasped the bow line. He knew he had to get into the boat but he must get rid of his heavy boots and sodden clothes to have any chance.

Frantically he began to work at the heel of one boot with the toe of the other. Water rushed into the boot, breaking the vacuum of pressure and it dropped away. The second proved more difficult but he floated on his back and tore it off beneath the boat, on the iron keel.

Without his boots the old man had more control of his movements and with one hand he pulled the canvas smock over his head and pushed it up over the boat side. His woolen jumper heavy with water was unmanageable and he discarded it and clung panting to the side of the boat. But he was ready.

He clutched at the gunwale, bracing himself for the lift, trying in vain to control his shaking limbs. He must get his head and shoulders into the boat, to have a chance of pulling himself aboard. Gritting his teeth he hauled himself up with all his strength. For an agonizing moment he hung there before slipping back with a cry of despair, into the water. He tried again and again until he could no longer bend his arms but only cling to the boat side, in desperation.

He looked up at his hands clamp-like on the edge of the gunwale shining, bone white in the mist. Big reliable hands as his fathers had been. Hands with a strength of their own to haul rope and fashion timber and make him proud and confident. They must hold for him now, he thought desperately, some how he must make them hold for him now. But he could only watch as one by one, his fingers lost their grip and his hands broke free and he slipped back into the sea.

The water closed around him, supporting his tortured frame and soothing his pain. He felt only relieve at the welcome embrace and turned slowly onto his back floating away from the boat on the still water.

Ola surfaced into a soft, rolling bank of cloud, yellow in the low sunlight. The surface of the sea was as quiet as mid-water and there was no wind. His signals ahead showed the cove where he had brought the seal, leading to the bay of man and his fishing grounds in the shallows. He slipped into the cloud and headed towards the land. It was here, in the swirling mist Ola came suddenly upon the boat. He sank at once beneath the hull; tail down scanning its smooth shape but there was no sound or movement. Slowly he rose to the surface and driving hard with his strong tail muscle he lifted his upper body clear of the water and circled, looking down into the boat. It was empty. There was no sign of man. Ola sank back into the water and dived, scanning the area around him. To one side, between the boat and the headland, he picked up another signal. It was on the surface, drifting with the tide and the trace was soft and misshapen. It might have been debris or floating weed, he could detect no movement but there was something. A faint bubble of sound and something else he recognized in a moment. It was the rhythmic beating of a heart.

His own heart quickened with the realization it was an air breathing creature and was neither dolphin nor seal. Cautiously he made a series of passes below the creature, sending hard contact signals to the surface. There was no response. Whatever it was, it seemed totally unaware of his presence. Curiosity finally overcame his anxiety and slowly Ola rose beneath the creature bringing it into view against the light. It floated above him, upright, like a seal, with only its head above the surface but as he moved closer, it extended long limbs towards him from the thin body, moving them weakly in the tide.   All at once he knew what it was. The creature before him was man!

For a moment he thought only of fleeing and putting as much distance as possible between himself and this man creature that had entered his world but it made no move in his direction and was clearly in a weakened distressed condition, perhaps close to death. He circled slowly, closer and closer, until his hard nose brushed an outstretched limb. There was no response but the movement of his great bulk below the creature, rolled it onto its face. Ola heard the choking gasp of water filled lungs as it tried to breath and a thin cordon of bubbles surrounded its head.

The dolphin responded at once, forgetting his fear of the creature. Without his help it was going to die. Grasping a limb firmly in his jaw, he rolled on the surface, dragging the man's upper body out of the water onto his soft stomach. He held it awash, secure between his pectoral fins, its head clear of any spray and broken water. It lay still making no effort to break free and Ola knew that like the young seal before it, if the creature slipped back into the water it would die. He began to swim slowly on his back, turning his head from side to side sending an arch of signals from the headland to the open sea. On the edge of the tidal race he found what he was looking for. It was the hard outline of the fishing boat floating in the mist.

The old man drifted in and out of a nightmare of consciousness and pain. Through salt encrusted eyes, he could barely see, nor had he the strength to lift his head, or truly comprehend his position but in one lucid moment he became aware of the creature that held him and for the first time in his life he knew naked fear of the unknown. He lay awash, on the soft underbelly of a dolphin rolling helplessly between great pectoral fins hard as bone that rose into the swirling mist, on either side. He could feel the power of the great tail muscle beneath him as the creature swam and an agony of pain from his left hand trapped in the creatures mouth. Through a thin veil of water the great jaw that held him, rose and fell before him, as the dolphin carried him seaward. As the boat loomed out of the mist ahead of him Ola swam alongside and turning onto his stomach released his charge, letting the man roll into the water. The creature floated alongside the boat but made no move to help itself. Gently Ola sank his great bulk beneath it and rose up lifting its limp body once more clear of the surface. Its breathing was shallow and laboured and it seemed unable to support itself but it was breathing. It was alive and he felt unable to leave it just as he could not have left the young seal to drown.

In the quiet of the mist, in a world that seemed to extend no further than the two of them and the empty boat, he waited for the old man to recover or die.

Consciousness for the old man, returned slowly with the sound of water around his boat and the creak of the rudder as the tiller swung. He floated free with just his head above the surface, resting on his arms. He no longer felt pain or cold, only a tiredness he might never wake from. The water around him gave him comfort and there was support beneath his chest and legs. Instinctively he reached down to lift himself further from the water and realization came swiftly as he felt the hard bottlenose and great head of the dolphin. In horror he tried to push himself away but there was no strength in his limbs and he slipped from the creature's smooth body into the water. The dolphin sank at once and rose beneath him, pushing him towards the boat. Instinctively he clutched one arm around the great dorsal fin for support and into his tired and tortured mind came the incredulous thought that the dolphin was trying to help, not harm him. It was a thought the old man could barely grasp.

He tried to open his eyes but his face was so badly bruised and swollen he saw the dolphin only as dim shape before him. He felt the timbers of the boat and stretched up a hand to the gunwale but he was desperately weak and it was beyond his reach. If he could lift himself on the dolphins back, he thought. If only he had the strength?

The thought that he might still have a chance to save himself but was too weak for the attempt, was almost as much as the old man could bear. He told himself he would rest and recover a little strength and if the dolphin would help him, he would climb back into his boat. He let his body slip down onto the creatures back, stretching out his arms and locking his fingers around its broad head, his cheek against its smooth skin and he prayed. Not to any God of man to save him but to this creature of nature that had delivered him so far. He prayed that it would stay on the surface beside his boat and give him one more chance to save himself... Just one more chance.

And he closed his eyes and slipped towards unconsciousness.

A popple of wind from the land, came to dry salt crystals in the old man's hair and blow tiny wavelets across the smooth surface of the water. It lifted the curtain of mist, freeing its grip on the land and drove it seaward and the bright sun that followed warmed the wind and the bones of the old man.

He woke and the brightness of the sunlight hurt his eyes and there was a taste of blood in his mouth but his mind was clear. He knew he was alive and the dolphin was still with him and what he must do.

Slowly and painfully, he lifted himself up on one arm and reaching down with the other, dragged a leg up in the water until his knee rested on the broad pectoral fin. The effort exhausted him completely and he collapsed kneeling forward over the dolphin, his face only inches from its breathing vent. The smell of stale fish on its breath enveloped him as he struggled to keep consciousness and hold his position. Slowly, with a great effort of will, he pushed himself upright and stretched out a hand again towards the boat. His fingers trembled with the effort and it seemed an age before they closed over the gunwale edge but inch-by-inch he pulled his body onto his knees and raised his head above the boat side.

He was so close. He needed only to get one foot on to the fin below him to push himself to safety. But all his strength was gone, he could move no further. As he knelt there and felt the pain return and grip his heart and the exhaustion drain his blood, the old man knew he was done and a great rage grew within him. He loosened his grip on the boat side and raised clenched fists to the sky. Head back and mouth agape he roared out in defiance of all that had caused his misfortune. But he could not hold himself erect for more than a moment and his body crumbled onto the head of the dolphin and the creature sank beneath him as if to carry him to the depths. His heart was bursting and the blood pounded in his ears as he felt the dolphin lift its head and drive with its great tail towards the surface. It rose out of the water in an explosion of power, driving him high into the air clear of the gunwale and tumbling his body into the boat.

Ola circled below the dark shape of the boat as it drifted with the tide. There had been no sign of movement since he had pushed the man creature out of the water and he could feel the gathering strength of the tidal race beneath him. He well knew that if the boat was carried into the turbulent water of the headland it would be driven onto the rocks.

Rolling onto his back he rose beneath the keel and spread his pectoral fins across the rough timber bracing his hard bottlenose against the bow. The way one dolphin would support another on the surface if it was injured or sick. Driving hard with his powerful tail he began turning the boat back towards the bay and calmer water. Almost at once he felt a change in the surface water around him. The tide had turned on the seabed below and as water lifted before the great rocks of the reef, pressure waves reached up to the surface, swirling into whirlpools and short breaking seas. The boat was almost torn from his grasp as it began to pitch and roll and the hard metal keel driven painfully into his soft belly. He needed all his power to hold the boat and swim against the tide but the effort was sapping his strength. He must break the grip of the race quickly, or let the boat go.

Almost at the point of exhaustion, Ola felt the tide weaken and the water around the boat, calm into a gentle swell. He was through into the quiet water of the bay and now he need only find a safe place for the man creature and he would be free of him. He surfaced beside the boat, pulling air into his lungs and stretching his pectoral fins and aching muscles. He searched ahead, probing until he found a break in the cliffs where a soft signal told him the water shallowed onto sand and shingle. It would do well enough. Ola slipped once more below the keel and slowly began to swim following the path of the signal towards the beach. Rocks came into view beneath him as the water shallowed, but he held his position beneath the boat until the last moment. With the shingle brushing his back and in danger of being stranded himself, he rolled clear, pushing the boat hard towards the shore. As he turned and dived away he heard the sharp keel strike the beach and the slither of stones and shingle as the boat came to rest. Ola rose to the surface, out of the dark shadow of the cliffs into the sunlight of the bay. A light offshore wind ruffled the water and lifted a gentle swell. It strengthened with the tide and carried him south clear of the headland. He was content to let the sea take him where it will. He wanted only to rest and recover his strength and leave the man creature and his world, far behind. Tail down and fins spread wide, he was quickly asleep and dreaming of his own kind, far out in the ocean, heading north... Coming home...

The old man felt the keel bite into the shingle and heard a rattle of small stones as the boat settled. He felt the warmth of the sun was on his face and opening his eyes, saw the hard edge of the gunwale and the cliff and a clear blue sky above him. He lay still and listened. Beyond the wash of the sea and the cry of gulls he heard a familiar sound. It was the squeal of a winch wire, running to the waters edge and the voices of the women folk gathering for the boats and the light step of small children on the shingle. He closed his eyes again to better hear the sounds and the image of his village, stretched before him. Stone cottages lay in the shadow of the cliffs high above the beach, and there was smoke over thatch and slate from every chimney and fishing nets draped the low sea walls, drying in the wind. At the waters edge, children ran in a flutter of laughter, around the skirts of the women folk.

It was good to be back, the old man thought. He lifted a hand to his face and opened his eyes. On the side of the boat above his head, perched a Herring gull snow white against the blue sky. It seemed to him close enough to touch and he reached out a hand towards it. But it spread its wings wide and lifted over him, circling higher and higher, out of the shadow of the cliff flashing gold in the sunset. His heart went with it, into the warmth of the sunlight and far below, the coloured sails of the fishing boats fluttered like butterfly wings in the evening light.

THE END